Where's Addie?

D1604867

Written by Donna Luber
Illustrated by Ryan Kennedy

Caritas
Communications

Luber, Donna

Where's Addie?

ISBN- 1537778196

ISBN- 9781537778198

Cover design by Ryan Kennedy.

David Gawlik
Caritas Communications
216 North Green Bay Road, Suite 208
Thiensville, WI 53092
414.531.0503
dgawlik70@gmail.com

I dedicate this book to my husband, children and grandchildren who give me great love and joy.

This is Mike.

He is a grown-up man, but ever since he was a little boy,
he has used a wheelchair because he was born with
muscular dystrophy. This means that he cannot move his
arms or his legs very well.

Even though Mike cannot walk, he goes to work every day.

How does he go places? Well, a driver takes him in a special van for people who use wheelchairs. That way he can go to work and he can visit the people who need him.

Mike went to school for many years
to learn to be a special kind of doctor who
helps people who have problems in their
lives. He also teaches in a college.
In his free time, Mike visits hospitals
and talks to people who have been
sick or hurt.

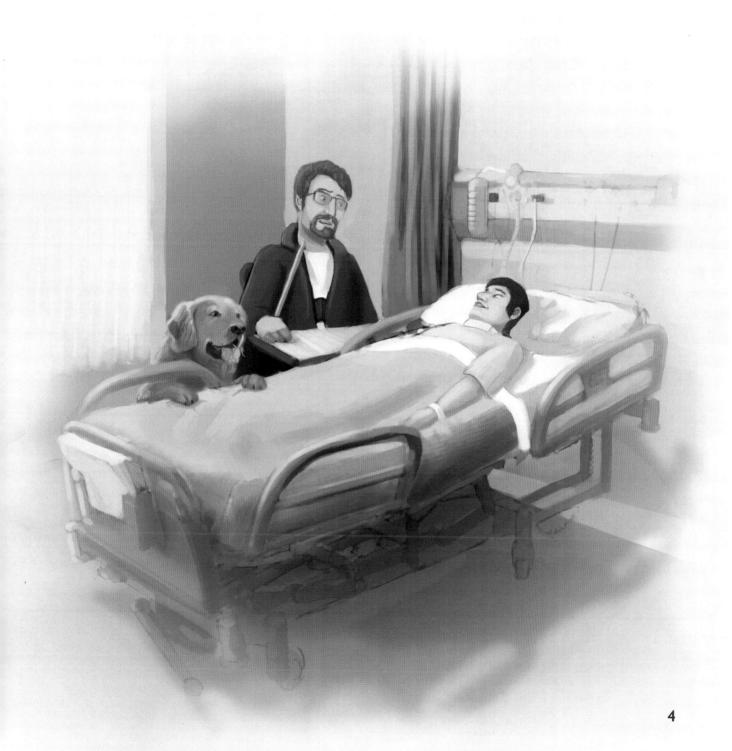

This is Addie.

She is a golden retriever dog.
She is twelve years old, and she weighs 60 pounds.

Addie is a very special kind of dog because
she helps Mike do things that he cannot do himself.

Addie went to a special school where she was trained to do
these things. She is called a service dog.

Addie can turn on the lights for Mike.

She can open doors for Mike.

She can pick up things and give them to Mike.

Addie is with Mike all the time, wherever he goes.

Addie has lived with Mike for ten years, since Mike was
a young man and Addie was a young dog.

They are best friends!

Although Addie is a very brave dog, she is afraid of one thing:
BIG STORMS.

When a loud rainstorm comes up, Addie runs into
Mike's closet or crawls under his bed to hide.

One Monday morning in July when Addie went outside
to go to the bathroom, a big storm blew in. Thunder
boomed and lightning flashed in the sky. Addie
became so frightened that she ran away!

Mike called and called, but Addie didn't come. Mike's Mom and Dad called for Addie, and his brother Scott called for Addie, but she didn't come home. Mike was very sad and so was everyone else who knew Mike and Addie - the mailman, the delivery man, and even all the neighbors.

12

The next day two men with cameras came from the TV
station to Mike's house. They asked Mike to explain to
people who were watching the news what had happened so
that they could help search for Addie.

Mike showed pictures of Addie
so people would recognize her.

He called the newspaper to put
Addie's picture in the paper.

Mike called the police department and the fire department and asked them to be on the lookout for Addie. He asked many mailmen if they had seen Addie running in the streets.

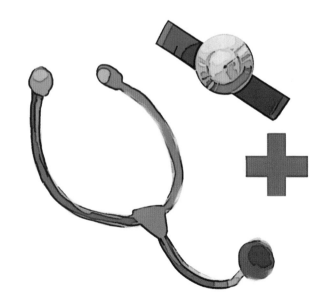

He called dog hospitals and the Humane Society to see if anyone had a dog that might be hurt.

Many kind people - even people he didn't know - came to Mike's house to help him look for Addie. Children arrived on bikes and rode around the neighborhood searching for Addie. Adults drove up in cars and motorcycles, and they rode around searching for Addie.

One man hired a helicopter and flew all over the
city to see if he could spot Addie from the sky.

People all over town searched under bushes, in garages, on beaches, in parks, and in yards. But no one could find Addie.

Mike had 7000 posters printed with his phone number and Addie's picture, in case someone saw her. The posters went up all over town - in grocery stores, in gas stations, in shopping centers, in veterinarian offices, and in many other places. A friend of Mike's family offered a reward of a $1000 to anyone who found Addie. But no one called Mike. Several days went by.

One day the Humane Society called to say that a golden
retriever had been brought into the animal shelter.

Mike grew very excited. How he hoped that this was Addie!
He went to the Humane Society, but the dog was not Addie.

A whole week passed and still Addie was missing.
A block away from Mike's house was a gas station.

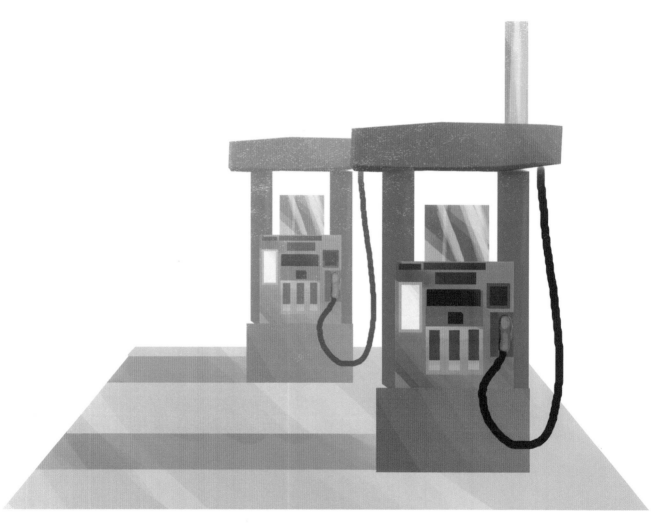

On Tuesday, Robert, the gas station owner's son, was fixing a van that looked very much like Mike's van.

When Robert finished his work, he crawled out from under the van. Lying right there next to him was a big dog, a golden retriever!

Robert's father recognized Addie and he said to
himself, "That dog looks familiar. She looks like the dog I saw
on TV and on the poster in my shop."

The dog's fur was matted with weeds and dirt, so the men cleaned her off.

The dog seemed very thirsty, so Robert and his father gave her four dishes of fresh water. The dog seemed hungry too, so they fed her four hot dogs from their own lunch boxes.

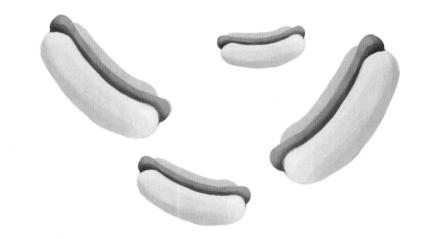

Then they called the phone number
that was on the poster. They told Mike
to come over and see the dog. Maybe it
was Addie. All the way to the gas station,
Mike hoped and hoped that
this dog might be Addie.

When Mike opened the van door, the dog leaped inside, jumped up on Mike's wheelchair, and licked Mike's face all over!

IT WAS ADDIE!
Mike was so happy that he couldn't stop smiling and hugging Addie.

Mike thanked Robert and his father again and again.
Then he took Addie to the dog doctor to be sure
she was not hurt or sick.

The doctor said, "She is just a little tired and a little thinner.
Take her home and let her rest."

When Mike was home, he called the TV station to report that Addie was home. The TV station sent a man with a big camera to report the happy news.

Later two more TV stations sent cameras to take Mike and Addie's picture. The next day the newspaper wrote a big article about Addie's homecoming.

Robert and his father donated their reward money to WAGS, the Wisconsin Academy for Graduate Service Dogs, the school that has trained Addie and hundreds of other dogs, to become service dogs that help people with disabilities.

To this very day, no one knows where Addie was for eight days. But Addie is back home and everyone is happy again - especially Mike and Addie.